JACK AND THE MANGER

JACK AND THE MANGER

by Andy Jones

Illustrations by Darka Erdelji

Running the Goat
Books & Broadsides
St. John's, Newfoundland

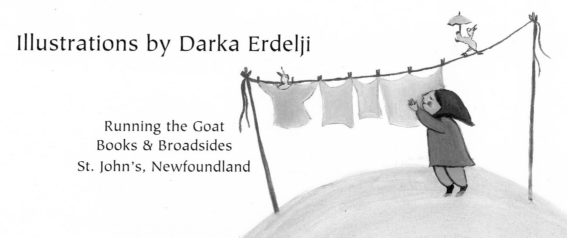

Now this story you may have heard, but this, we'll say, is from a different point of view…. Now once upon a time in olden times, it come to pass that there was a mighty emperor, and his name was Caesar Augustus.

Now when he was a youngfella, this Caesar Augustus, he went to the circus one time with his Uncle Julius, and at the circus he had to guess how many gumballs was into an urn … a big jar—about that size … and he guessed it right and he won the gumballs. But, ever after he had had to know *how much of everything was into everything*. If he passed by a henhouse he had to know how many chickens was inside. Then, his servants'd have to go into the henhouse and count all the chickens. And if he passed by a pond he had to find out how many fish was into it—then they'd have to drain the pond and count the fish. He had everybody drove!

And when he grew up and become emperor—same thing. He'd ask his servants, "How many olives do you suppose is in that barrel?" And they'd say, "Oh, there's thousands, b'y," and he'd say, "No, no, *exactly* how many olives is there?" And they'd have to empty out the barrel and count em. They'd say, "Augustus," they'd say, "we should be growin olives, not countin em."

Anyway, whatever way it was, one day the emperor got to wondrin: "How many people," he wondered, "is in my empire?"

Well, his servants tried ta fob him off by sayin, "There's *millions*, b'y!" and leave it at that. But that was no good for Gumball (that's what they called en, now, behind his back—'Gumball'—like they say the servants in Buckingham Palace calls the Queen 'Brenda' behind her back. Oh yeah, that's apparently her 'below-stairs nickname,' you might say).

Anyway, we're talking about *Gumball* here. Gumball had to know how many—*exactly* how many—people was in his empire.

So one of his servants suggested he send somebody out with a piece of paper and an abacus (that's what they called a calculator back then) to write down all the names and add them all up.

But the emperor said, "Ohhh, no," he said, "that won't work with the crowd out east, cause they're always workin in the oil fields in Egypt somewhere …" (That's the olive oil fields—there was a real oil boom on in them days.) "… and they're always comin home holiday time, and runnin off to the next settlement to visit this or that cousin, so you can never pin em down to count em."

'Til one of his servants suggested, "You make a decree," he said,
"that everybody got to return to the town they were born in, and they
got to stay there 'til they're counted."

And somebody else suggested, while they were there why not tax em!

So that's what he done, and so it come to pass that the Emperor
Caesar Augustus, he give out that everybody was to return home
to the town they were born in to be counted and taxed. And I spose
that was the first 'Come Home Year.'

And that's where this story begins … and before you know it
there were people going up and down every road in the land
from where they was at, a'wards where they was born to.

And walkin down one of those roads was a very famous person.
You probably know the name—yes, that's right, his name was Jack,
and he was from a town called the Mount of Pearls, which was just
outsida Bethlehem. Now some people just called it 'the Pearl,'
but anyway that's neither here nor there. Much like the Pearl.

Now while Jack was walkin along on his journey home, he met
a young couple—man and a woman, them days—on the road,
and they were goin into Bethlehem proper, and since it was
        on the way, Jack and they figured they'd travel together.
            And that's what they done.

Now the woman, she was very young, and the husband … well,
    he was a bit older. And the woman was quite talkative.
        Oh, she loved a chat. She could talk the sleeve out of a coat,
            like they used to say. But the husband, he never said
                very much.

Now it was a long walk and a'wards the end of the first day
Jack ends up walkin alongside the young woman—if I recall correctly
her name was Mary, but that's neither here nor there. Nor were they,
for that matter … I mean, you know, they were still on the road.
Anyways, he was talkin away to Mary—she was leadin a little donkey,
I think, and she said, she said to en, she was with child, she was
gonna have a baby.

And Jack said, "Well," he said, "I figured you was,"
he said, "but I didn't like to say anything," he said,
"cause sometimes you says that and the missus
is just a little on the chubby side, and then
you are in trouble."

She laughed and said, "No, no, I'm with child, and he's due to be born any day now."

"Yes," says Jack, "I can see that." And anyway they kep on talkin and after a while she said, "This child," she said, "is gonna be special!"

"Yes, ma'am," says Jack, "They're all special, them youngsters."

"No, no," she said. "I'm talkin about something different. Come closer," she said, "I'm gonna tell ya something. An angel," she said, "appeared to me and told me this baby was a boy and he was gonna be a kind of king who was gonna introduce the best kind of love and peace into the world."

"Well," laughs Jack, "that's a different kinda king than I ever heard of!" Then, thinkin that his laugh might have seemed harsh, he says, "Anyways, Missus, look, I got no reason to doubt what you're sayin, you seem like an honest young woman."

But tell you the truth, Jack was a bit uncomfortable with all the 'angel talk' and so he changed the subject, and he said, "Your mother and father must be happy about the baby—li'l grandchild an all."

"Ohhhh, yes," she said, "they're over the moon altogether. This is their first grandchild and they're both in their 80s."

"What!" says Jack. "You're so young! Shur that's impossible!"

"No, it's not," she said, "cause I got to tell ya,"—she was whispering now—"a couple of angels appeared to them and told them that even tho they were old, they were gonna have a baby …
and that baby was me!"

Anyway, it was gettin duckish, and the three of em turned in for the night. They went into a little gravel pit by the side of the road to camp. (Oh yes, gravel pit campin was still legal then—Gumball didn't have his fingers into every pie.)

Now, by gar, the second day Jack found hisself walkin alongside the husband. He didn't know the husband's name, but they got to talkin, they were havin a grand chat, and he seemed like an ordinary Joe, 'til he pulled Jack aside and said, "Jack, b'y, I got to tell ya something."

"Oh, yeah," says Jack.

"I'm bustin," he said, "to tell somebody cause it's on me mind.... "

"Oh, yeah," says Jack.

Jack was figurin he'd hear the story of how the youngfella was gonna be some kind of king and was gonna introduce the best kind of love into the world, which, to tell the truth, Jack wouldna minded hearin again.

But no, the husband says, "I'll tell ya something now," he says: "That young woman there is my wife."

"I know that," says Jack.

"*But*," the man says, "the child she's carryin *is not mine!*"

"Ohhh, yeah?" says Jack, not feelin all that comfortable, and kinda wishin now he'd set out alone.

 "But ..." says the husband, "... *I don't mind.*"

"*Ohhhh, yeahh?*" says Jack.

"Yes," says the man. "I *was* upset, but, ya see, an angel appeared to me ... " ("Ohhh, yes," says Jack to hisself, "another angel!") "... and the angel told me that the baby come to be *by the work of the gods own power*, and that the baby born was gonna be very special, was gonna show the world the way to peace and the best kinda love."

"Well," says Jack, "spose I can't argue with that."

And 'fore you know it, night was upon them again.

And it was a cold, cold night, and they were just
comin into Bethlehem, and Jack was just gonna take
his leave of the young couple when Mary, the young woman,
turns shockin pale and she says, "Oh, my," she says, "the baby's
comin!" and the husband says, "We got to find
a place for to have that baby," and Jack says,
"Never you mind," he says,
"I knows lots of people hereabouts.
I'll get you a hotel room."

And he goes to a buddy of his who works at the Bethlehem Hotel
on the Fair Mountain, and his buddy says, "Jack, b'y,"
he says, "there's no place to stay here.
We're full up cause of Emperor Gumball's
count-and-tax plan. Even the boiler room is full!"

Then Jack goes to another buddy of his who works at a travelers inn,
where you can tie up your donkey outside, right next to your room,
and lo and behold *they* got no place to rent; so Jack goes back to Mary
and her husband and says he can't find nothing, but "if you can walk
a bit further on," he says, "you can stay at my basement apartment
in the Pearl."

But then, oh, it becomes obvious, they ain't gonna make it—
that baby's comin fast!

So Jack runs up to a nearby farm house and the farmer, well,
he's a little suspicious, but he lets em all sleep in the stable,
and before you could say 'Bob's yer uncle' that sweet little youngster
was born, and they wrapped en in swilin clothes, and after he was
plimmed to the gills with milk, he was a'lied right down in the manger
where the cows would normally eat their hay. Little boy, he was,
like was predicted by at least *three* angels; and the youngfella's fine,
no problems. The father wanted to call en 'Ralph,' but the mother
said, "No," she said, "he's meant to be called 'Yeshua'." ('Jesus,'
we call it now.)

And when Jack looks at that young babby, he got to admit there's
something special about the little fella. And he's moved....
Yes, Jack is *struck*, and he says, "I got," he says,
"I *got* to go spread the good news."

And so he goes out.
Now he remembered he seen
some shepherds on the way,
so he figured he'd round em up
and bring em into the stable,
but lo and behold, he walked down
the lane a few steps when he met
the shepherds comin a'wards *him*!

He said, "Hang on where yer to, fellas. Where ya headin in such a hurry?"

And they said, "We're headin a'wards the star!"

"What star?" says Jack.

"Look up," says the shepherds. And whatdyaknow, but Jack looks up and there was this star ... oh my, oh my, oh my ... this star'd practically knock the eyes right outa your head—and it was *right over the stable*.

And he said to the shepherds, "How'd you know about this?"

"Well," they said, "an angel appeared to us...."

"Ohhhh, yeah," says Jack.

"Yes," says one of the shepherds. "The angel came down and he said, 'Fear not,' he said, for I gotta admit," says the shepherd, "a mighty dread had seized our troubled minds when we seen that angel; but the angel said to us, he said, 'down in David's town this night is born a special baby that's gonna show a guaranteed way to peace-on-earth-and-the-finest-kind-of-love-among-humankind' **aaand** that the above-mentioned baby was gonna be wrapped-in-swilin-clothes-and-in-a-manger-laid *in this very stable*!"

So the shepherds goes into the stable, and, well, Jack he figures he'll sneak off now, home to the Pearl. But he's hardly out the door when, lo and behold, he meets three fellas decked off in king costumes! Oh, my! He figured they must be mummers. But guess what? Turns out they *are* kings, and they're after coming from the farthest corners of the earth.

And Jack says to them, "Don't tell me," he says, "an *angel* told you to come here."

"Not eeeexactly," they said. And then, whispering, they told Jack, "But an angel *did* tell us not to tell the local governor, an awful fella by the name of Herod, that the baby was here."

"That's good advice," says Jack, "cause when Herod hears about this little fella, he's gonna wanna have him made away with!"

"That's exactly what the angel told us!" said the three kings.

And Jack shows the b'ys into the stable, and he notices each of em
got a lovely gift with em, a Christmas box I guess you'd call it now,
and Jack, he figures he'll slip away without sayin a word, but he takes
one last peek inside. And, oh my, oh my, oh my, what a lovely sight.
As pretty as a picture, it was, like a Christmas card—the mother and
the father, a crowd of animals, a fair flock of shepherds, three kings,
donkey, and a lovely baby who is, by all accounts, *eventually* gonna
guide us all towards peace on earth.

I can hardly wait.

And you know it was twelve years later, when Jack was working as a janitor up to the temple, that a youngfella come up to him, taps him on the shoulder, and says, "Jack!"

Well, Jack turns around and looks at the youngfella, but he's not sure who he is.

The youngfella says, "I'm after hearin a lot of stories about you, Jack!"

And Jack stands there for a moment, and then it dawns on him. "Jesus," he says, "oh, I'm after hearin a lot of stories about you, too! How's your mom and dad doin?"

"Oh, finest kind," says Jesus, "but they're proly looking for me right now. I come in here," he said, "and I got lost."

"Lost in the temple," says Jack, laughin, "oh my, oh my. I'll show you the way out."

And on the way out, Jesus says, "Well, Jack," he says, "I, ah, I heard ya climbed a beanstalk!"

"No, no, no, that's totally exaggerated," says Jack.

"But ya did jump over the candlestick?" says Jesus.

"Yes," says Jack. "I done that. And I shipped to a cat aboard a canoe, for a year and a day ... but that's *a long story*."

Now they made their way outside, and there was Mary and ... Joseph (it turned out was the father's name). Well, they couldn't thank Jack enough for finding their youngfella and Jack reminded them, he said, "You got," he said, "you *got to let him go*; he got to be about his famous business!"

And Mary said, "How do you know that, now, Jack?" and Jack said, "Well," he said, "an angel appeared to me."

"What?" says Mary and Joseph together.

"No, no," says Jack. "I'm only jokin!"

And they all had a grand laugh, and remembered back to the trip
they had to Bethlehem, and the shepherds and the angels and the kings
and the manger and the donkey and the star and the wonderful chats
they had on the road, and how it all just seemed like a dream …
and Jack invited them if they were ever in the Pearl, they could stay
in his basement apartment. Then he turns to the youngfella and says,
"We all got high hopes for you buddy, but don't go startin no
organization, cause they'll just arse it up."

Jesus laughs and says, "I'll do me best."

"You better," says Jack.

And then, the youngfella puts his hand on Jack's shoulder and
I swear—you can slit me throat, you can cut out me liver if I tell
a lie—every bit of arthritis was in Jack's shoulder was gone!

Now, granted, he had taken some medicine that morning,
but whatever way it was, I know this story is true cause Jack
hisself told me and I wrote it down. At least I think it was Jack.
Maybe it was an *angel*. It's all a bit hazy....

But what odds, I don't have to know *everything's that's into everything*. I'm not Gumball! And I know that nobody's interested in the gospel accordin to me, or accordin to any of ye, for that matter. But that is the end of my story. And I suppose

Peace on earth has not been found,
Yet it seems we know the way.
And if we ever get there
We can well and truly say,
It might've begun with that tiny Babe
Who was born on Christmas Day.

Jack and the Manger is the second in an on-going series of Jack stories, featuring retellings and adaptations by Andy Jones, and illustrations by Darka Erdelji. The first, *The Queen of Paradise's Garden*, was published by Running the Goat in 2009.

The narrative voice in this story was inspired by the oral traditions of Newfoundland and Labrador. It is especially indebted to the storytelling style of Freeman Bennett, of St. Pauls on the Great Northern Peninsula; Pius Power Sr. and his family, of South East Bight, Placentia Bay; and Anita Best. To honour these people and the other storytellers who have shaped his love of storytelling, Andy Jones has ignored some of the strictures of formal written language, choosing to participate instead in the energy of the dialect and the verbal traditions of this place. He has tried to capture the cadence of the language with punctuation and a sentence style more musical than grammatical.

This story was inspired, in part, by Jonathan Goldstein's retellings of stories from the Bible, and by Mary Walsh and Cathy Jones's "Deb and Sheila" sketch: Andy thanks them very much. He thanks as well Mary-Lynn Bernard, and those three other lively listeners down the lane—Alice, Edward and Walter Ferguson-O'Brien.

While working on this story, Andy served as Writer-in-Residence at Memorial University of Newfoundland and Labrador, in St. John's. He thanks the University community, and especially the members of the Department of English, for their warm welcome. He is also grateful to Kay Anonsen and the City of St. John's Arts Jury for support during the writing of this book.

Darka Erdelji thanks her family in Slovenia—Vlado and Martina Erdelji, Jana Erdelji, Mateja Kolenc, and Niko Erdelji; and her friends—Sasha, Marion, Monique, Madonna, Karen, Frederique, Marnie, Lidya, Willow, April, Andy, Melanie, Fionulla, Michelle, Geoffrey, Paul, Erin, Susy, Megumi, Donald and Janet, and Donald and Phoebe.

She is also grateful for the support of the City of St. John's Arts Jury and the Newfoundland and Labrador Arts Council.

An acclaimed actor, writer and storyteller, Andy Jones is from St. John's, Newfoundland.
He has had a long career in theatre, television and film. His other children's books are *Peg Bearskin*
(co-written with Philip Dinn) and *The Queen of Paradise's Garden*. Andy is a contributing author
to *The Plays of Codco* and *Three Servings*, and is the author and narrator of the audio book
Letters from Uncle Val.

A native of the former Yugoslav Republic of Slovenia, Darka Erdelji graduated with a Masters of Arts
in Puppet Scenography from the Akadmie Muzickych Umeni in Prague in 1999. Since moving
to St. John's with her partner and children, she has worked building puppets and sets for, and
performing, puppet plays; illustrating books; and creating ceramic artworks. She collaborated
with Andy Jones on the puppet play *The Queen of Paradise's Garden*, and illustrated the book of the
same name.

The typeface is Tiepolo; it was created at AlphaOmega Typography for the International Typeface Corporation in 1987. The papers are Rolland Natural.

Designed by Veselina Tomova of Vis-à-Vis Graphis, St. John's, Newfoundland. Printed by The Lowe-Martin Group, Ottawa, Ontario.

978-0-9737578-9-7 (paperback)

978-0-9866113-0-8 (hardcover)

Running the Goat
Books & Broadsides
8 Mullock Street
St. John's, Newfoundland
A1C 2R5

www.runningthegoat.com